This
MOUSE ▦ WORKS
Classics Collection Storybook

belongs to

Mickey's the Mouse

Pinocchio

Pocahontas

Beaty and the Beast

~~*Ka Zoua Her*~~

Kaab Zuag Hawj or
Kuang Zoua Her

Aire

Caterpillar

© SmileMakers #NATU

Princess Power

xoxox

Disney's

OLIVER
& Company

On a spring morning, the streets and sidewalks of New York were crowded with hurrying people. But on one quiet corner, someone had left five homeless kittens in a cardboard box. Taped above them was a sign that read, "Kitties Need Home."

The kittens peeked hopefully out of the box. They were so cute that one passerby after another stopped to pick up a kitten. Finally, there was only one left.

5 KITTIES
NEED HOME

No one had taken the fluffy orange kitten, and he felt lonely and afraid. He was hungry, too. Timidly, he climbed out of the box to look for something to eat.

Whooosh! Huge cars and trucks whizzed past, and giant feet brushed by him. The blaring street noises—honking horns, clattering wheels, loud radios—hurt his ears. This was no place for a kitten!

But then, a delicious smell reached him. It came from Louie's hot dog cart. And around the corner came a dog named Dodger, who had a good idea about how they could get some of those hot dogs for breakfast!

"In this town," Dodger advised the kitten, "you have to be smart to get by. Let me show you how it's done."

With that, Dodger started to growl and snap at the kitten, chasing him toward the hot dog cart.

The kitten ran straight up Louie's back!

"*Ouch!* Get out of there!" yelled the angry Louie, as the kitten dug his tiny claws into Louie's neck. Meanwhile, Dodger helped himself to a string of hot dogs!

Then the clever dog made his escape with the hot dogs draped around his neck like a necklace. The kitten was right behind him, leaving the angry hot dog seller shaking his fist at them.

"We were a pretty good team," the kitten said to Dodger. "When do we eat?" But Dodger had made up his mind not to share his prize. Suddenly, he raced away!

"Wait for me!" cried the kitten. "Half those hot dogs are mine!"

But Dodger only laughed and called back, "Sorry, kid! You're on your own now!"

Speeding through narrow alleys and over fences, the street-smart Dodger was sure he had lost his small friend. When he got down to the docks, he disappeared into a rundown barge.

Aboard the barge, Dodger's gang greeted him eagerly: Rita, the elegant Afghan hound; Einstein, the Great Dane; Francis, the bulldog who wanted to be an actor; and tiny, nervous Tito, the Chihuahua.

"Hey, Dodger fans, it's time to eat," said Dodger proudly, as he gave out the hot dogs. Then he began to brag about the fierce monster he'd had to fight to get them:

Meanwhile the kitten, out of breath by now, had tracked Dodger to the hideout and was leaning through a hole in the deck to listen.

Suddenly the kitten leaned over too far, and his small furry form tumbled down among the startled dogs!

The gang surrounded the frightened kitten and glared at him. He said in a shaky voice, "I was just following this dog..."

Tito snarled, but Dodger
backed up the kitten's story.
"It's true," he said. "So, kitty—
what took you so long?"

The kitten's little heart was
pounding.

"Relax, kid," said Rita.

The kitten finally spoke up.

"I helped you get those hot dogs," he said angrily to Dodger. "And I want my share."

Just when it looked like a fight would break out, a man dressed in old patched clothes came in with a box of dog biscuits. The gang rushed to greet him.

It was Fagin, the scrap collector, and he looked worried. Proudly, Einstein displayed the collection of junk that the gang had rounded up from the city's trash cans that day. But even that didn't cheer Fagin up.

"Sykes will be here any minute," he announced, as the gang tried to get him to play. Then the loud blast of a car horn outside made him jump. "I'll be right there!" he called out.

But before he could go out to the dock, Sykes's two fero-cious guard dogs burst into the room, showing their great gleaming teeth. Growling, they pushed Fagin aside and made for the kitten, who hid behind Dodger. The guard dogs closed in, but Dodger stood his ground.

"Nice doggies," said Fagin nervously, slipping out the door as one of the Dobermans snapped at him.

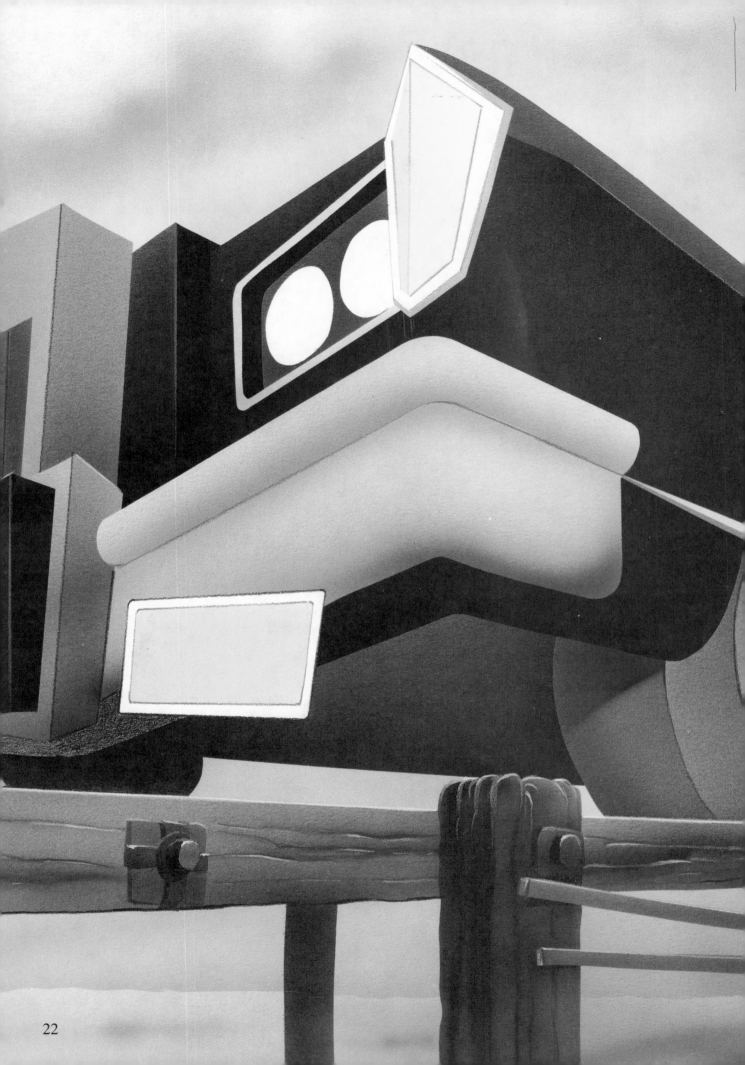

Trembling, Fagin stood on the dock beside a huge black limousine and handed in what the dogs had collected. A harsh voice said, "I don't want junk!" and a cloud of cigar smoke blew into Fagin's face. "You've got three days to get the money you owe me," said Sykes. "Or else!"

Sykes whistled to his dogs, and the limousine roared away.

Inside, the gang was admiring the brave kitten, who had scratched one of the Dobermans on the nose.

When Fagin came in looking blue, the gang tried to cheer him up, but it was no use.

"Three days," said Fagin, near tears. "I never should have borrowed that money."

Suddenly Fagin brightened as he remembered something. "Who scratched that Doberman on the nose?" he asked. Gently, Dodger pushed the kitten forward.

"You!" Fagin laughed, picking up the kitten. "That took a lot of guts! We never had a cat in the gang before, but..."

The gang barked approval for the kitten's adoption.

Worn out by his troubles,
Fagin fell asleep as soon as he
had read the gang a story. The
kitten curled up comfortably in
Dodger's bed, very glad that
he'd found a home.

The next morning, Fagin woke up in better spirits. "Let's go!" he said, and the whole gang climbed into a battered three-wheeler and took off with a roar. Bouncing and jouncing, they headed for the city.

They were a motley crew, with their ears flying in the wind. Excitedly, the kitten hung on, sure that the day would be full of adventure.

The kitten was right. Fagin had a plan, and Dodger explained it while Francis and Einstein went down the block and hid behind a building.

"It's car radios we're after today," said Dodger. "They'll bring a good price for Fagin. Watch how we do it."

The bulldog and the Great Dane took up their positions near a traffic light. When it turned red, an expensive-looking limousine pulled to a stop, and Einstein threw himself against it. Then he let out a series of loud yelps, as if he'd been hurt. The limousine's driver jumped out to see what had happened.

Meanwhile, Einstein had slipped away, leaving the talented actor Francis in his place. Francis waved all four feet in the air and cried pitifully, convincing the poor driver that he was hurt. The driver was so upset that he didn't see Tito, the technical wizard, jump into the limousine and start to work on the wires under the dashboard with his teeth. The kitten was to keep watch, but he got so nervous that he stumbled onto the ignition key and gave Tito a terrible shock!

Tito gave a loud screech, and Winston, the driver, rushed back just in time to see the little dog leap out. Forgetting all about the radio, Tito ran for his life, leaving the frightened kitten in the car. In the back seat was a little girl, who reached over to pick him up.

"What a sweet kittie!" the little girl cried happily. "You're coming home with me."

By this time, Winston was very confused by all the animals he'd seen in the last few minutes.

"Why, Miss Jenny, where did you find that cat?" he asked.

"He's lost," replied Jenny, "and we're taking him home with us."

As the limousine rolled away with the kitten, the gang stared after it. "Tito, you were supposed to keep an eye on him," snapped Dodger.

"Well, it's hard to watch anything when you're getting fried!" Tito replied angrily.

At home—a handsome town-house on Fifth Avenue—Jenny prepared a huge bowl of food for the kitten.

"I'll take good care of you," she told him.

Unfortunately, Jenny had served the kitten's food in her prize poodle's dish, and the poodle, Georgette, was very annoyed! With her stylish topknot quivering, she stalked into the kitchen and growled, "Cat! Do you have any idea whose bowl that is?"

The kitten shrank away, but Jenny ignored the poodle's jealousy.

"Oh, Georgette, this is my new kitty," said Jenny. "I'm going to call him Oliver."

Jenny and Oliver sat down at the piano and she made up a little song about him, while Georgette sulked. "Why should that cat get all the attention?" she muttered.

Jenny's parents were away, but she assured Oliver that they would love him, too. He felt very lucky to have been adopted twice in two days!

But Oliver's friends had not forgotten him. The next morning the gang watched Jenny leave for school. Then Francis lay down on the steps and played dead, while Einstein rang the doorbell.

When Winston came to the door and saw the limp bulldog, he shouted "You again!" Francis got up and raced down the street. While Winston was yelling after him, the rest of the gang ran into the house.

The house was like a palace to the dogs. "Wow!" said Tito. "How bad can this place be?"

But Dodger was not impressed. "We came here to get our cat," he said. "Let's go!"

Upstairs the gang met Georgette, who was lounging on pillows near her elegant canopy bed. The gang liked the poodle's style, and Georgette was more than happy to lead them to Oliver.

Sleeping peacefully on
Jenny's bed, Oliver didn't know
that his friends had come to
rescue him.

"Is this the kitten you want?"
asked Georgette.

"That's him," said Dodger.
Then the gang scooped Oliver
into a pillowcase and left by the
fire escape.

"Jenny will get over this," thought Georgette smugly. "Good riddance!"

When the gang got back to the barge, they let Oliver out of the sack.

"You're home now," said Dodger proudly.

"But I...I was happy there," said Oliver.

The gang was surprised to hear this, and they were looking at each other, puzzled, when Fagin walked in. "Only one more day..." he muttered.

Then Fagin noticed Oliver and picked him up. "Thought you'd left us, kitty," he said. Oliver was wearing the gold tag that Jenny had put on him the day before, and Fagin studied it closely. "Eleven-twenty-five Fifth Avenue," he read aloud. "So that's where you've been—where the rich people live!"

Fagin's face brightened. Maybe there was a way to get the money he owed Sykes, after all!

Surrounded by the eager gang, Fagin sat down with pencil and paper. After chewing on the pencil for a while, he began to write: "Dear Mr. Very Rich Cat Owner..."

Then Fagin brought Oliver to Syke's warehouse in the shipyard—a dark, creepy building where the gangster had his office.

"So, Fagin," demanded Sykes, "have you brought my money?"

"Sykes," stammered Fagin, "I have an air-tight kitty—uh, plan, airtight plan!" He put Oliver down on the desk and explained that he had found a kitten belonging to someone rich. The owner would come to the dock that night to pay a high ransom for his pet.

"Okay," agreed Sykes. "But this is your last chance."

Fagin waited nervously for Oliver's owner, holding the bewildered kitten behind his back. Finally, Jenny appeared, followed by an unhappy Georgette.

"Excuse me, Sir," said Jenny to Fagin. "I'm looking for my stolen kitty. I brought *this* to pay his ransom." When she held up her piggy bank, Fagin felt ashamed. He couldn't go through with his plan.

"That's funny!" said Fagin, producing Oliver. "I just found this lost kitten. Is he yours?"

"Oh, Oliver!" cried Jenny, taking him in her arms. "Thank you, Mister!" Oliver purred as loudly as a kitten could.

Unknown to the three on the dock, Sykes had been watching from his limousine. Realizing that he could get a much higher ransom for Jenny than for the kitten, he roared up the alley and snatched the child into the car. Poor Oliver was left behind, as Fagin chased after the limousine shouting, "You can't do that!"

Aboard the barge, the gang heard the yelling outside and rushed to investigate. "Jenny!" cried Oliver. "He took Jenny!"

"Don't worry," said Dodger, with a reassuring wink. "We'll get her back." Georgette agreed to help, and they set off for Sykes's warehouse at a run.

The gang was in luck. Sykes was busy on the telephone, trying to reach Jenny's parents to demand a ransom. With his back to the TV monitors, he didn't see the gang slip into his hideout.

Tito, the wiring expert, began to shut down the electrical system, while Einstein locked the door to Sykes's office!

But the gang had forgotten about Sykes's secret weapon— the powerful Doberman guard dogs. On his shouted orders, they began sniffing around the warehouse, searching for the intruders.

Meanwhile, the gang had crept along a catwalk to the room where Jenny was tied to a chair. Georgette gazed happily at Jenny as the others worked to free her from the ropes.

Suddenly they heard the Dobermans barking nearby!

Then Tito spotted a way out.
He sped up to a platform
where a large crane controlled
a hook hanging from the
ceiling. Quickly, Tito began
to rewire the control box,
which lowered the hook
toward Jenny's chair. Dodger
attached the hook to the
chair and ordered, "Quick,
everyone, climb on!"

Just as the chair rose
toward safety, Sykes burst
in with an axe in his hand,
followed by the snapping
Dobermans. Sykes struck a
control panel with the axe, and
a burst of electricity threw Tito
from the platform. The chair
crashed to the floor, scattering
Jenny and the gang.

Everyone scrambled to his feet and headed for the loading door to escape. Imagine their relief at finding Fagin outside on his three-wheeler waiting for them. "Get on!" he cried, and Jenny, the dogs, and Oliver piled onto the motorcycle and sped away.

But Sykes had leaped into his limousine with the Dobermans and was quickly gaining on them. Desperately, Fagin
bounced down the subway steps and onto the platform.

But when he looked back, he found that Sykes had followed them and Fagin was nearing the end of the platform!
He jumped the three-wheeler onto the tracks, but Sykes
stayed right behind him.

"Help!" yelled Jenny, as Sykes rammed the back of the motorcycle. She was thrown onto the hood of his car, and his hand reached out to drag her inside. But Oliver wasn't about to give Jenny up. He bit Sykes's hand as hard as he could.

Sykes screamed with pain and yanked his hand in, throwing Oliver into the back seat with the Dobermans! Fagin gave the wheel to Georgette and pulled Jenny back onto the three-wheeler, as Dodger sprang to Oliver's rescue.

Dodger's attack sent the surprised Dobermans crashing through the back window. One fell to the tracks and Dodger fought the other on the car roof, where Oliver joined him. Then Dodger and Oliver saw Fagin swing out onto a bridge. Sykes followed.

When Fagin saw that the end
of the bridge was blocked off,
he swerved wildly to the right.

Behind him, Sykes slammed on his brakes, but it was too late. Dodger and Oliver jumped off the limousine just as it drove off the bridge. Jenny hugged Oliver tightly as the big black car disappeared. That was the last anyone saw of Sykes.

The next day, Jenny invited the whole gang to her birthday party. Winston and Fagin drank sparkling soda, to celebrate Jenny's return, while Jenny and the gang—including Georgette—had plenty of ice cream and cake.

Tito and Einstein agreed that the new friendships they'd made were worth all the trouble they'd been through. And Jenny said she already had her birthday wish: "Oliver and all of you, safe and sound."

Happy to leave Oliver in
such a good home, and
promising to visit, the gang
headed back to the
city streets they loved.
Hopping a ride on a
passing car, they made up
a wonderful song about life
in New York City.

ISBN 1-57082-044-9
10 9 8 7 6 5 4

Oliver, Company